For Harry Hendy Butcher

HOUSE

Ben's Big Book of Cars

A HUTCHINSON BOOK

Published in Great Britain by Hutchinson,
An imprint of Random House Children's Books

PRINTING HISTORY
This edition published 2002

1 3 5 7 9 10 8 6 4 2

RANDOM HOUSE CHILDREN'S BOOKS
61–63 Uxbridge Rd, London W5 5SA
A division of The Random House Group Ltd

RANDOM HOUSE AUSTRALIA (PTY) LTD
20 Alfred Street, Milsons Point, Sydney,
New South Wales 2061, Australia

RANDOM HOUSE NEW ZEALAND LTD
18 Poland Road, Glenfield, Auckland 10, New Zealand

RANDOM HOUSE (PTY) LTD
Endulini, 5A Jubilee Road, Parktown 2193, South Africa

THE RANDOM HOUSE GROUP Limited Reg. No. 954009
www.randomhouse.co.uk

A CIP catalogue record for this book is available from the British Library.

Printed in Singapore by Tien Wah Press [PTE] Ltd

BEN'S BIG BOOK OF CARS

Ben Blathwayt

HUTCHINSON

London Sydney Auckland Johannesburg

All Kinds of Cars

Three-wheeler
Two wheels at the back and one at the front

Saloon
A smart car to drive to work

People carrier
Enough seats for a big family

Estate
Lots of room in the back

Van
For small deliveries and light loads

Hatchback
A smaller version of the estate car

Four-wheel drive
The engine controls all four wheels so it is easy to drive over bumpy ground

Convertible
The roof can go up or down

Pick-up truck
Strong enough for tough use

Sports car
Goes very fast!

On the Road

Roundabout

Horse box

Flyover
A road that goes
over the motorway

Embankment

**Electronic
sign**

**Crash
barrier**

Cattle bridge

Caravan

Police car

Emergency telephone

Hard shoulder
Cars can only stop on the motorway if they break down

Taking a Break

Fuel pump
To fill up the tank

Air
For the tyres

Oil
For the engine

Water
For the radiator

Service station

Check the engine

Car wash
For a clean, shiny car

On tow
A broken-down car being towed to the garage

Exercise
To stretch stiff limbs

Car park

Café
Help yourself to a hot meal

Picnic
Bring your own snacks

Shop
For gifts and refreshments

At the Garage

Scrap metal
Can be melted down and used again

Workshop
Where cars are repaired

Waste oil
Can be used again

Breakdown truck
To tow broken-down cars

Tool chest
Holds all sorts of tools

Oil can
Stops squeaks!

Socket set
Unscrews bolts of all sizes

Fire extinguisher
For putting out a fire

Spanners
Tighten and unscrew bolts

Oil drum
Keeps oil safe

Vice
Tightly grips objects

Hydraulic ramp
Lifts cars up high

Inspection lamp
Aims light into dark spaces

Trolley jack
Holds the car up while the tyre is changed

Parts of the Car

Starter motor
Gets the engine running

Battery
Provides electricity

Distributor
Sends electricity to all the spark plugs

Sunroof
For hot, sunny days

Windscreen
Must be kept clean

Bonnet

Carburettor
Mixes the fuel with air

Wing mirror

Engine
The heart of the car

Air filter
Keeps the carburettor clean

Wheel
Moves the car along

Spark plug
Sparks a little explosion

Pistons
Make movement for the wheels

Shock absorber
Helps stop bumpy rides!

CAR 02 01

Fuel tank
Stores the fuel which powers the engine

Headlight
Helps drivers see at night

Exhaust pipe
Carries away poisonous fumes

Gearbox
Holds the gears which change the speed of the car

Hubcap
Covers the centre of the wheel

Steering wheel
Turns the car to the left and right

Disc brake
Slows and stops the car

Tyre
Grips the road and helps stop skidding!

Radiator
Cools the water that stops the engine overheating

First Cars

Panhard-Levassor, 1901
The Panhard-Levassor was one of the first cars to have an engine at the front, a gearbox, four wheels rather than three and a proper steering wheel.

Model T Ford
"Tin Lizzie", 1908

Bugatti Type 35, 1924

Early cars were very expensive, difficult to drive and unreliable. In 1908 Henry Ford designed a car that everyone could afford. His factories produced over 23 million Model T Fords.

Some drivers wanted only speed and excitement from their cars, others were happy with comfort and reliability.

**Rolls-Royce
Phantom II Continental, 1929**

Cars that Race

Dragster
Very noisy and very fast

Go-cart
Small, low to the ground and lots of fun!

Stock car
Specially adapted for rough racing, these cars often crash!

Sports car
Sports car races can last a whole day and night

Touring car
Ordinary cars with specially tuned engines to make them go fast!

Rally car
Must be strong enough
for the roughest of tracks

Grand Prix racer
A magnificent racing
machine with a big engine,
big tyres and a long,
smooth body

Rally Car Racing

Splashing through water

Bouncing over bumpy ground

Rally cars race one by one over a course that is often narrow and rough. The fastest time wins!

Skidding on snow

Speeding round corners

Grand Prix Racing

Grandstand

Footbridge

Control tower

Hairpin bend

Pit

Crash

Pit stop

Loudspeakers

Track marshals

Getting ready to race

Out on the circuit

Into the pit for more fuel
and a quick tyre change

Super Cars

Lamborghini Countach
For very rich people!

Ferrari F40
One of the fastest cars
in the world

Jaguar E-Type
Named after a wildcat

Morgan Plus 8
Every car is handmade

Porsche 911
Some people's dream car

Classic Cars

Popular in their day
and still seen on
the road today!

Morris Mini Minor

Very small and easy to park

Volkswagen Van

The whole family can go on holiday

Volkswagen Beetle

Designed by Ferdinand Porsche

Austin Healey "Frogeye" Sprite

A classic British sports car

Citroën DS "Décapotable" (convertible)

Stylish, with a special suspension

Morris Minor
Very reliable

Morris Minor Traveller
Reliable with lots of room

SAAB 96
Designed for the cold Swedish winters

Ford Escort RS
Won lots of rallies in its time

Citroën 2CV "Deux Chevaux" (two horsepower)
Ideal for getting the wind in your hair!

Fiat 500 "Topolino" (little mouse)
A perfect, little, city car

Unusual Cars

Locomobile Steamer
Many early cars were powered by steam

Solar-powered car
The glass panels turn sunlight into electricity

Amphibious car
As happy in the water as on the road

Impact
This electric car runs on batteries which need to be recharged every day

Thrust II
A jet-powered car taking the old land speed record at 633 miles per hour

"Stretched" Limousine
Often carries famous people!

Trojan Bubble Car
A tiny, three-wheeled, novelty car

Lunar Rover "Moon Buggy"
The first car on the moon!